Acknowledgements

I'd first like to thank my family for reading through the different drafts and giving me advice. I'd like to thank my editor, Liz Shine and Red Dress Press, who's input was monumental in bringing the story and characters to life. I'd also like to thank any friends and family who gave input on cover design and my sister, Melissa Even, for designing the chosen cover.

Before Plagues

Standing on tiptoes, Madu reached for a plum, smooth and fragrant, placing it in a small basket. She smiled. The first of the plums were ripening, and many more were on the way. She saw her twin brother, Nour, making his way towards the house. She waved at him, excited to show him what she picked.

Madu was an eleven-year-old girl in a working-class family in ancient Egypt. Nour attended scribe school in order to potentially boost his social status over their parents. He told Madu that he wanted to put his studies to use someday, but Madu had a feeling that he wasn't sure as to what that would look like. He talked about the census, copying religious texts, and more extensively, not having to pay taxes. Madu hoped he would find something that brought him joy.

Madu envied him a little. Girls very rarely became scribes. She loved the thought that any idea she had could be put right on a papyrus for anyone even hundreds of years later to see. Not only that, but she could read ideas of all sorts of other people with their own things to say!

She may not have had much knowledge of hieroglyphics, but she could paint. She had a mural on her roof that she would occasionally add to. One could tell what mood she was in by looking at parts of the painting. Sometimes, it was specific content. Other times it was in the subtle details, like how tall the trees were, how calm the river was, or the splashes of color. It also could have been that Madu remembered painting it and the mood she was in.

Her parents, Selma and Osaze, had both come from poor families, so they too were expected to live as peasants. They were fortunate enough to have things a little easier. Under a better economy, Osaze could take up pottery and spend a little less time in the fields. Sometimes, he'd let Madu paint designs.

Madu's youngest brother, Jabari, was six and had the brightest smile. There was great talk a year and a half ago of whether to send him to school. Osaze argued that they should give him the same opportunity as Nour to advance his standings. After seeing the long hours Nour spent and how stressed, exhausted, and beaten he got, Selma didn't think it was necessary, especially when things were looking up.

The kids would help with the crops when needed. These days could go a little long every so often, but the work wasn't too strenuous. During the flooding season, the Nile engulfed the banks, and farmers didn't need to work. During the agriculture season, cattle would plow the fields, and the kids would follow planting the seeds. They would use a shaduf, a large pole balanced on a cross-beam to water the crops. On one end was a rope and a bucket, and on the other a counter-weight. The rope was pulled to lower the bucket into the water. Then, someone else pulled the weight to raise the bucket, which would be swung around to water the crops. During the harvest season, they used curved, sharp sickles to cut tall grains. Cattle trampled the cut corn to remove grain from the ears.

As Madu was now eleven, she was expected to marry a respectable husband in not too long. The thought of getting married delighted her! Her parents had introduced her to a few nice men already. Madu was excited to see what would happen and move into a new stage of her life.

She would often spend the day looking after Jabari. Selma explained that Madu would soon enough have her own children and should be prepared. Madu; Jabari; their cat, Sanura; and Jabari's friend, Jumoke, were out playing. A small bird flew by, and Sanura jumped. The boys got on all fours, pounced at the air, and landed like her.

"Do you think she's trying to catch the bird?" Jabari wondered, watching it fly away.

"What do you think she was going to do with it?" asked Jumoke.

"Maybe she saw a pretty puff in the air and was curious."

"Maybe she wanted to be friends."

Madu smiled. She didn't feel the need to tell the little boys that Sanura hunted small birds to consume and devour.

"Catch!" Behind her, Omorose, another child who lived nearby, threw a ball. Madu instinctively turned, stepped back, raised her hands, and caught it. Omorose burst into giggles, spreading to Jabari and Jumoke then to Madu. Omorose whispered something in the boys' ears. They all took off.

"You can't catch us!" Jumoke teased.

Madu ran after them. Up ahead, Jabari sprinted towards the Nile and jumped in. They splashed Madu, who splashed them right back. They all laughed. Sanura stood at the shore, amused.

Madu had one of those rare opportunities on the roof to paint. Nour was at school, Osaze was at the market selling pottery, Selma was meeting with a potential suitor, and Jabari was with friends. Madu was sure her parents wouldn't be especially excited about her being on the roof. Madu had been up plenty of times and trusted her footing.

Madu painted as she felt compelled in the moment. She may not have had a grand, long-term plan, but when she stepped back to admire the mural, it came together so well. She added some streaks of dark purple to the rich blue river. The sky was a fainter blue with hints of red. Near the front, she added a darker brown to the cat's hair and gave the fur some texture. She added a small grey shape fluttering away. Along the shores grew green thin-leaved papyrus. On the other side of the river, kids ran and climbed trees. Behind them were rows of houses she imagined being filled with happy families. Birds flew in the sky and rested on the river.

Climbing down, Madu ran into her friend, Kesi.

"I've been so busy," she told Madu. Kesi was Omorose's older sister. Their family were peasants. "We've been doing fine though, there was plenty left over for us."

"Good to hear," said Madu. "My mom's meeting with a suitor."

"What do you know about him?"

"Well, his mom makes jewelry. His dad weaves. I've heard he's a very nice young man."

"My parents have met with a few men. They're still discussing who they like best," Kesi explained.

"Any in particular who stand out?"

"I haven't spent a whole lot of time with any of them. They all seem fine. I don't know; I guess I'll just trust Mom and Dad's judgement." Kesi shrugged, giving a slight smile.

Madu looked down before meeting her eyes. "Are you nervous?"

"That they'll pick the wrong person?"

"Or moving out of the house and spending the rest of your life with them?"

"Yeah," Kesi agreed. "when you're little, you think people old enough to get married have everything figured out and be ready for anything. Then, your own parents are looking for suitors, and you realize you aren't even close."

Madu nodded. "if that's how you define adulthood, I don't think anyone's really an adult."

Kesi smiled. "yeah, true."

"I was going to make some bread for dinner. Would you like to help?" Madu asked.

"Sure!"

Osaze prepared some corn, and Selma finished a fresh batch of beer. The family was seated at the table for dinner.

"So you had that test you've been studying for," Selma noted.

"Yeah, it went a bit better than expected, but I'm glad it's over," said Nour, putting his head on his hand.

Jabari dropped a few pieces of corn in front of Sanura, who had been looking at him.

"Maybe now you'll get a little time to relax," said Selma.

Nour looked down at the table. "Yeah, a little."

Selma turned to Osaze. "I met with Ebo. He seems like a good match for Madu. I told him you could meet tomorrow afternoon."

"Sounds good," said Osaze. "How's his price?"

"He comes from a merchant family, so they're willing to pay well."

"So you think it's going to be him?" Madu asked.

"I like him. He's definitely in the running," Selma answered.

Selma liked him, which meant that soon enough, Osaze would meet him. What if they both liked him, and they introduced him to Madu, and he and Madu liked each other? She might be getting married soon! It might not be him, though. Her parents might decide to keep looking. She might not click with any of them right away. She couldn't get her hopes up too much in case she was disappointed. She also had to prepare herself in case things worked out.

Blood

Selma opened the door to find Bes, a family friend, looking panicked and exhausted. "Tough day of work?"

"Unlike any other day I've ever had!" Bes replied. He sat down and looked up as everyone focused on him. "We're in so much trouble! Some dirty Hebrew possesses some dark magic, magic that Egyptian magicians can't undo! He threatened Pharaoh, saying that if he didn't free the Hebrews, he'd turn all water into blood!"

Oh dear.

"A few of us took notice and were alarmed by the threat. Then, Pharaoh started laughing, so we felt reassured. Then, the Hebrew proved he could do it!"

The family sat in silence. Pharaoh couldn't let this happen! He cared for the Egyptian people! He fought for the Egyptian people! Before Madu was born, her family were peasants. After the Hebrews started working as slaves, life became a bit easier. Money became a little less tight, and it was a little less difficult to put food on the table. With less time working the fields, Osaze was able to take up pottery. People wanted to buy his work. He found himself relying on his craft for income and worked in the fields much less.

Osaze couldn't imagine going back to supporting his family merely as a peasant. Bes' family would have an even worse time. Pharaoh wouldn't allow his own people to struggle and sink. He was looking out for them!

How dare the Hebrew God ruin their precious Nile!

Madu went outside to see for herself. Sure enough, the Nile was bright red, and the smell was nauseating. How was anyone going to survive?! The thought made Madu's throat drier.

All they had was what could be dug up. They strained the sand, but the water was still brown. They added crushed Moringa seeds. When they decided the water was clear enough, they strained the seeds. The volume had shrunk considerably.

"How long do you think things will be like this?" Nour asked as they got ready to sleep.

"It seems indefinite," Madu responded. "If Pharaoh's not going to set the Hebrews free, do you think we'll ever get our water back?"

Nour paused. "What do you think he's going to do?"

"He's looking out for us. He can't let us go without water. But he also won't let us starve without a roof over our heads." Madu didn't know any Hebrews personally. All her life, they had been kept as slaves. That was just how it was. It was a good thing, she had been brought up to understand, as it would otherwise be her own family and friends laboring all day, barely able to feed themselves. Their lives depended on keeping the Hebrews in slavery.

She couldn't blame them, though, for wanting freedom. As terrible as their action was, Madu couldn't help but realize that deep within the hostility was self-defense. The Hebrews were trying to get out of the exact position that her family was trying to avoid. If Pharaoh were to set them free, their own grim, unbearable future would be the same as what the Hebrews were already living. Either stance she could take provoked unshakeable discomfort.

"They've been slaves for decades," Nour said. "Letting them go now would dismantle everything."

At last, a group came by with carts full of canisters of water gathered from the Red Sea .

Selma picked up a fairly medium-sized canister. "This much for this amount of water?" She and Osaze exchanged glances and shrugs.

"Would it be more expensive to get one larger canister or multiple smaller ones of the same volume?" Osaze asked.

"Multiple small canisters," a woman answered.

"Smaller would be better. If one of them spills, it's not all the water," Madu added. "Of course, we could just separate the water ourselves."

"What's the next size down?" asked Selma.

Their eyes shifted from the canisters to each other.

"This is more in our price range," Osaze observed, "but we need more water than this!"

"The first one, then?" Selma asked.

Osaze nodded.

After the transaction was completed, the kids were invited to each take a sip.

People were growing more frantic each day. Everyone seemed to think that Moses and his God were going to back down at some point, but there wasn't time to sit and wait. The last few days were spent digging, searching for whatever might be in the ground. Selma, Osaze and many others refused to give up. Madu started to doubt Pharaoh a bit. She thought he should try to reason with Moses. Maybe he could make conditions a little bit better for slaves in exchange for giving them some water back? She hoped Pharaoh had a plan. He must have a plan!

A few days later, nothing had gotten better. Madu asked Kesi if she thought Pharaoh was doing enough.

"He's doing as much as he can," Kesi replied.

"I don't know if he is," Madu confessed.

Kesi gave her a blank look. "What can he do? Magicians don't have the power to undo the curse! What else is there?"

"He can try to reason with the Hebrews."

Kesi raised an eyebrow. "You think that's a good idea?"

"I think it's the only option," said Madu.

"And let them win!?" said Kesi, eyes widening.

"They've already won! Pharaoh can at least partially meet some of their demands or we'll continue with things the way they are! They've trapped us! Pharaoh has to come to terms with that!"

"I don't know why you're telling me this. I'm not Pharaoh. Whatever it is he should be doing, it's not up to us."

She wasn't really wrong. It was ultimately Pharaoh's responsibility. He was the one who called the shots. He was the one with power. Still, the idea that all she could do was watch and wait didn't sit right.

Frogs

Madu awoke to loud croaking and a splash of slime on her face. Then, another on her knee. She felt something small, wet, and slippery being hurled and deflected from her skin. They were all over the room! Small, warty brown frogs sprung from wall to wall. Spotted green frogs larger than her fists hopped across the furniture. She'd never seen so many at once. She couldn't imagine what had brought them into her house.

The family got to work trying to get rid of them. Sanura tried to pounce on them. Madu would use a box to catch the frogs but only a few at a time. Every time they were released, more came in.

They weren't just in the house. There were swarms as far as Madu could see! People outside tried just as hard to shoo them away.

"Why is this happening?" Jabari wondered, shielding himself with a chair.

Nour stopped swatting, seemingly in thought. "Because all bodies of water turned to blood, they must have been drawn away."

"But the water turned to blood a week ago! Why did the frogs only come today?" Jabari asked.

"They were probably confused at first," Madu answered, "maybe it took all week for them to perceive what happened."

Nour nodded. "Interesting, I thought that any consequence to come we would have already experienced."

"Who knows what more could happen!" said Madu.

"Enough!" Selma covered Jabari's ears. "Do you have to have this conversation in front of him? You two are scaring your poor little brother!"

"I've already been scared, Mama, ever since a week ago when the water turned to blood."

That afternoon, a messenger came to the neighborhood. "We've been blessed with a miracle!" He announced. "Seven days ago, the Nile along with every body of water in Egypt turned to blood. This was done by a Hebrew man blackmailing Pharaoh into freeing the slaves. As of this morning, every body of water has been switched back to normal!"

Cheers and gasps were heard in the crowd.

"This hasn't been done because Pharaoh gave in to the Hebrews demands, but by the work of the gods. Unfortunately, the story's not over. The Hebrew man approached Pharaoh once again to ask to let his people go. This time, their God sent frogs!"

Madu sat down with Ebo. He'd hit it off with both her parents, so the two of them had been planning to meet. They had to postpone because he was ill, but Ebo was feeling better.

"So your parents are merchants?"

"Yeah, my mom's a jeweler, and my dad's a weaver. I've learned from both of them, so I guess I'll do a little of each. Your dad's a potter?"

"Yeah, I've painted some of his work."

"Really! They didn't tell me you painted!" said Ebo.

Madu blushed. "It's not really something I do a lot."

Ebo turned his attention towards the dishes on the counter. "You're good at it. The designs are so pretty!"

"Thanks!"

He took her hand.

A frog knocked over the canister of water. Thank the gods that could be replaced! Sanura grimaced as the frog lept away.

"Has she caught many?" Ebo asked.

"Only a few, but she does her best."

"My cat, too."

Sanura sat next to them. Ebo pet her. "What's her name?"

"Sanura."

"That's lovely!"

"Does your cat get as ticked off by the frogs as she does?" Madu asked.

"Oh yeah! They zigzag all over and so many are constantly coming in and out of view!"

He seemed nice. They chatted a little while longer and agreed to meet again.

For the third time in a row, Madu awoke to a chorus of groans. Not that she had gotten much sleep. They never went away. Day and night, they sprung all over, croaking in everyone's ears.

Still, it was better than the blood. Excitement of having water again overshadowed annoyance over the frogs. Even Madu felt like frogs were only a minor inconvenience in the grand scheme of things. Since all the water was back, would the frogs be temporary, too? Of course, they would only be replaced with something else. But frogs aren't as bad as blood, so it's not like each plague would necessarily be worse than the last, just different.

Madu spent the afternoon caring for Sanura, who was sick with salmonellosis from the frogs. She had a fever and an unusually fast heartbeat. She was always tired and dehydrated. Madu tried to keep the frogs away from Sanura for the time being by hanging up some rugs, but there were always some able to get through. Plenty of people and animals had gotten sick these past few days.

As she was getting water, Madu ran into Nour and his friend, Sabra, studying hieroglyphics. "How's she doing?" Nour asked.

"Sanura still seems to be in a lot of pain."

"Her, too? It keeps popping up everywhere!" Sabra commented, looking up from his work. "Between the three of us, I don't think our worry should have ended when the water turned back."

"I guess this is how things are going to be from now on, one horrible event after another," said Nour.

"Until Pharaoh finally agrees to free the slaves," Sabra remarked.

"You think he's going to?" asked Madu.

"He'll have to eventually," Sabra reasoned. "As soon as he does, our lives will finally go ba-"

"They won't go back to normal!" Nour told him, fist on the tabe. "Without Hebrew slaves, people in lower classes will fall deeper into poverty! Our family and many others will have to struggle to get by!"

"Aren't we already?" Madu said.

"The frogs are bothering them just as much as they're bothering us. At some point, they'll see we mean business and stand down," explained Nour.

"Maybe, but if they're going to continue sending plagues until someone gives in, might as well be sooner than later."

The group consisted of Madu, Nour, Jabari, Sabra, his sister, Hasina, Kesi, and Omorose gathered around the table at Sabra's house.

"So we've established that something needs to change, but there's no obvious solution," said Nour.

"The easy solution to each problem just makes the other worse," explained Madu.

"What did you say? It's a little hard to hear over the frogs," Omorose yelled.

"I said, 'the easy solution to each problem makes the other worse.'"

"There's got to be a way to compromise," Kesi suggested. "Maybe Pharaoh can at least make conditions a little easier for slaves in return for plagues that aren't quite as bad."

"I agree. They should talk things out like mature adults and come up with a solution that works best for everyone instead of stubbornly holding their ground while people suffer," said Hasina.

"I bet the frogs have a harder time getting into his palace than into our houses," said Jabari.

"He also doesn't have to work the fields when he's sick," Madu added.

"Who gets punished for poor harvests!? Certainly not those at the top," said Omorose.

"Doesn't seem like someone with personal servants and buckets of jewels who attends banquets every week is the best person to make decisions for the poor," Nour said.

"That's why he needs to hear from us," Madu decided.

When Madu tried to paint, the frogs had proved as much of an interference as she predicted. They spilled two bowls and tracked paint everywhere! Madu would have to wait.

She found Sanura in the same corner Madu had left her behind the rugs. Madu brought her more food and water. Sanura ate and drank a little, but for the most part, she hardly moved. She felt warm when Madu pet her.

"My first memory was when Dad brought you home," Madu recalled. "Nour and I were so excited! You were so cute and shy. We crazy three-year-olds weren't exactly calming."

Sanura purred. She shut her eyes. She lay still as Madu felt her speeding pulse.

"You would try to pounce on anything in front of you. Birds, frogs, garlic."

Madu watched Sanura's breath rise and fall.

"You were always so puzzled by the odd child things we did, like pretend to be tables, dance with geese, dress you up like a princess. You sure put up with us!"

Her pulse had slowed down.

"Whenever I was sad, you would sit in my lap and I would pet you. You might act disinterested, but you were there."

Madu couldn't find her pulse. Sanura's breath had stopped rising and falling.

Getting ready in the morning, Madu dipped her hand in the mud and gently spread it over her head and face. She glanced at Sanura lying next to her empty coffin. After all these, today was the day she would move on.

The family made their way to the Nile, where they were greeted by friends and neighbors in blue and grey. The women's faces were covered in mud, and the men's eyebrows were shaved. She spotted Kesi, who gave her a hug.

"She was a good cat," said Kesi.

Madu nodded. She knew cats died of
salmonellosis. She'd been taking care of Sanura for a few
days and could tell she wasn't doing well, but Madu
thought she would make it. She had in mind a
miraculous, unexpected recovery.

She was too young to have much memory of her
grandma's funeral. As they boarded the boats for the
ceremony, west of the Nile became much more real. The
frogs were loud, slimy, and annoying, and had taken out
the most sacred of animals.

At last, they reached the tomb, and Sanura was
placed in her coffin for the Opening of the Mouth
ceremony.

She saw Ebo exit one of the boats. "You came!"

"Of course I did. Sanura made a good impression."

"I'm glad to hear that!"

The priest got the crowd's attention. Two women
stepped up, representing the goddesses Isis and
Nephthys.

"Come to your house, come to your house!" Isis
chanted, "you of On, come to your house, your foes are
not!"

Madu held her brothers' hands as the women
recited the Lamentations of Isis and Nepthys. She took in
every line and each part of Sanura's body the priest

touched as she regained touch, taste, smell, hearing, and sight to use in the next life.

Lice

Madu awoke to quiet. For the first time in two weeks, she bathed and felt properly clean. She scratched her head and took in the astonishing peace. She knew what this meant, but with the weight of her loss and the ease of the break, she wasn't ready to worry about the next catastrophe. She knew that this moment wouldn't last forever, but it was here now.

Madu poured herself some beer and sat down for breakfast. She scratched her head.

"So what's this club you three are starting?" Selma asked.

"A group of us are getting together to discuss how we think Pharaoh should be handling slavery and the plagues," Nour explained.

Osaze scratched his head.

"It's just seven of us right now. We're going to need more support to make a difference," Madu said.

"The plagues might be over now," Osaze told them.

"Maybe," Jabari replied.

"The frogs were crystal clear before we even knew the water returned to the rivers," Selma said.

"But we didn't know about the blood until Bes told us," Madu countered.

Nour and Jabari were both scratching their heads.

"It seems silly to worry about something you don't even know is here," said Osaze.

"We'll notice something eventually," said Jabari.

"We aren't going to convince anyone if everyone thinks things are back to normal!" Sabra cried.

"It's weird; the chaos really seems to be over!" Omorose commented, scratching her head.

"It doesn't make sense! Moses tells Pharaoh that he'll send a new plague every time he refuses to free the slaves, but we haven't seen any signs of the slaves being freed nor any new plagues!" Madu recapped.

"It almost feels pointless to talk about," Nour admitted.

Kesi scratched her head.

"Maybe we should just enjoy ourselves for now," suggested Hasina.

The group decided to let off steam by playing a game of floor hockey. Sabra and Hasina had gotten their siblings, Hathor and Kafele to join, and Jabari had recruited his friend, Jumoke. Kesi took the puck from Kafele, shot it right past Sabra, and scored.

"You could have blocked that!" Nour yelled.

"I'm sorry; I had an itch," Sabra explained.

"You snooze, you lose!" Kesi teased.

Madu raised her hand to scratch her own head and was startled to catch Jabari, Jumoke, Hathor, and Omorose all doing the same. "Seems like we've been doing this a lot this morning."

"What?" Kafele asked.

Hasina scratched her head.

"Even before we met, our family was scratching their heads all through breakfast," Madu observed.

"Maybe I should check your hair," said Kesi.

"All of us should check each others' hair," Madu said.

The group had formed a circle and were carefully examining each others' scalps.

"I think I saw a bug!" Nour hollered. "It disappeared very quickly, though."

"Looks like you've got some, too!"

"Were they in any other household before we met up?" Madu inquired.

"Maybe," Kesi answered.

"We should go around and see if anyone else has this problem," Sabra advised.

"Why?" Hathor asked.

"Because we've suspiciously not noticed a new plague," Hasina answered.

"I don't especially care for politics, but you guys have fun!" Kafele told them.

Madu, paired with Jabari, set out to investigate the neighborhood.

"Hi, my name's Madu. This is my brother, Jabari. We live about fifteen khets away. How are you?"

"Fine, I guess. What brings you over?"

"Our plum tree's doing so well this year that we have more plums than we can eat! Would you like one?" Jabari offered.

"Sure." The woman took one, scratching her head. "You guys are lucky to have such an abundance!"

"Is that vase from my dad? It looks like something he would make," Madu observed, gesturing behind the woman to vase with red leafy designs.

She gave it a brief glance and scratched her head. "It might be. I've had it so long, I don't remember."

"Is your head itchy?" Jabari asked.

She looked at him and lowered her hand. "Yes, I've had a bit of an itch all morning."

"Ten for ten," Jabari muttered.

"Thank you, you've been helpful!" Madu and Jabari moved on to the next house.

"It's not something I've really thought much about."

"Well, it's an issue that's been seriously threatening us these past few weeks, and will continue if we don't do something," Hasina explained.

"Starting this afternoon, we'll be holding daily protests outside the palace," said Madu.

"You guys are awfully ambitious!"

Kesi and Omorose were working, and Nour and Sabra were at school. This left Madu, Hasina, Jabari, and Jumoke for recruitment. The responses weren't exactly what they'd been hoping for.

"You guys are so cute wanting to help out, but also so young. Let the adults handle these sorts of things."

"You think you have all the answers?"

"It's just lice! Your generation's so entitled!"

"You two young women should be out looking for husbands. You boys should wait until you're older and wiser to go around stating what Pharaoh should do."

"Don't worry! Go out and play! Enjoy your time being young and carefree!"

"You think your problems are greater than ours?"

"It's all a hoax!"

A small handful of people they recruited showed up. Sabra and Nour had managed to convince a few of their classmates. Government officials did take notice.

They received looks of disgust and also some of surprise, maybe even intrigue.

"Every week, a new disaster challenges Egypt. We don't know what's to come, but until Pharaoh does something, new dangers will continue to threaten us! No one should have to choose between an endless lifetime of plague after plague and a risk of falling into poverty! The fact that so many families are stuck relying on the backs of Hebrew slaves, people we once welcomed with open arms, and feel like they have no choice but to turn a blind eye to lice rising from the dust of the earth; loud, slimy, dirty frogs covering every square shezep; and every source of water turning to blood tells us that there's something deeper going on. I know my friends and family wouldn't justify these beliefs unless they had to!"

Filling in for her dad at the market, Madu so far had managed to sell five bowls and three vases.

"Hello," a young woman about her age approached, scratching her head. By now, people knew what was going on and weren't trying to play it cool. "You were at the palace! You were the one who made that speech!"

Madu blushed. "You were there?"

"Yeah, I thought it sounded amazing. My name's Rabiah."

"I'm Madu, nice to meet you!"

"Your speech was quite something!"

"Thanks! I think," Madu replied.

"You're quite the visionary! Too bad you're not Pharaoh!"

Madu sighed. "things would be different."

"Listen, I agree with your message, but I don't think you'll get anywhere demanding the world. At least for now, asking for Pharaoh to free the slaves and stop the plagues is enough."

"No, that won't work." Madu turned to help the next customer.

"Really? I think getting Pharaoh to agree to one thing would be easier than getting him to agree to two."

"Except that these aren't two separate issues. If Pharaoh frees the slaves and ends the plagues, those of us in the lower class would have a much harder time getting our basic needs met."

Beasts

Madu heard the buzzing and felt them on her skin. When she finally opened her eyes, she wasn't surprised to see swarms of flies, mosquitos, and hornets. The fact that lice were out of her hair didn't make up for being bitten and stung. Then, she heard a growl. Out the window, Madu saw wolves, bears, and snakes.

"We have to stay inside all week, don't we?" Jabari asked.

"That's hardly going to help," Osaze told him. "If we lived in a big, expensive house, we'd be much better off."

They pushed all the furniture to the windows and door. They used Osaze's clay to fill in the gaps.

The family had been sheltering for a few hours when something came wriggling through the cracks. The snake had light brown striped scales and a horn above each light brown eye. Jabari threw an onion at it. The snake bared its fangs and slithered towards him. Nour pulled some chairs away from the door, leaving an opening. As they escaped, the family caught the attention of a wolf. It wasn't enough for them to split up because that wolf wasn't the only one.

Selma grabbed the edge of a window and climbed onto the roof of a house. Osaze and Nour made it up the other side, and Madu helped Jabari. The wolf was at her heels by the time she started climbing. She had an incredible stroke of luck to get both legs up on the roof! As she did, she heard a growl followed by a cry below. Madu was surprised to notice her parents and brothers looking down not in horror, but in awe. The wolf was lying on the ground with an arrow in its side. A man holding a bow-and-arrow aimed at another wolf. The wolf who had chased them moved its legs a bit and looked around. Cautiously, the wolf got back on its feet and pounced on the man.

Madu and Osaze kept watch while Selma, Nour, and Jabari slept. She did her best to resist scratching her bug bites. Her stomach grumbled. She heard faint sobbing. "Jabari?" she murmured. Jabari was sound asleep. In fact, no one else had woken up; it was her dad who was crying.

"I don't know what to do!" Osaze muttered. "Things are bad. Things are real bad!"

"I know," Madu replied.

"We can't constantly be running for our lives! I don't know how we're going to keep going all week!" Osaze lowered his head, forehead resting in his hands.

Madu leaned closer and gave him a hug. "I wonder how our friends are doing. I hope they're okay."

"Maybe we will have to return to our lives as peasants," Osaze admitted.

"You think Pharaoh's going to set the Hebrews free?"

"With things the way they are, he'd be crazy not to."

"Yeah," Madu really hoped he was right.

It was barely dawn when Selma shook Madu awake. "Run! Now!" Somehow or other, a bear had gotten onto the roof! Madu was about to jump but saw a wolf below. She ran to the other side and started up immediately after landing on her feet.

"Madu!" Jabari was ahead. She sprinted after, hoping Nour and their parents were near. She zipped around a colossal snake in her path and lost sight of him.

"Right!" Nour yelled. Madu turned. She couldn't see much in front of her besides the swarms. Behind, she heard running and panting. Luckily, it was Nour, catching up. "Where'd he go?"

Osaze grabbed her hand and pulled her away. "In here!" One wall of a house had some bricks that had gotten loose, leaving a hole just large enough to fit through. Selma was already inside, and Nour trailed close behind. A man holding a baby and a woman hugging a toddler huddled in the middle of the room.

"Fill that in as quick as you can," the man instructed.

"Where's Jabari?" Selma demanded.

"He was way ahead. We lost track of him." Nour and Madu picked up the loose bricks and patched up the hole.

"He can't still be out there!" Selma cried.

"I can't imagine how I'd be feeling if Latif or Pili were on the run without us," said the woman. "My name's Lapis. This is Latif, baby Pili, and my husband, Chibale."

"I'm Selma. This is my husband, Osaze and my kids Madu and Nour. Jabari's my little one."

"Is that a hole in the floor?" asked Nour.

"We spent all morning digging yesterday. We've trapped a wolf and six snakes," Chibale explained.

"Don't go too close," Latif warned.

Madu's stomach growled.

"Would you like some bread?" Chibale offered.

"Thank you. I would love some. We haven't eaten since yesterday morning."

The family devoured their pieces of bread. They could only hope Jabari was safe.

The bear's head emerged through the hole with two outstretched arms. Everyone leapt towards the opposite wall. The bear struggled, but the hole wasn't wide enough.

"Do we have any way of killing it?" Nour asked.

"Poke it with a big stick," Latif suggested.

"Too bad all the loose bricks are over there," said Osaze.

"Here's a knife we use to cut meat. Is there something I can attach it to, or should I just throw it?" Lapis asked.

"I say throw it," Chibale pitched.

The blade hit smack in the left eye. The bear wailed and struggled to wriggle free. Finally, it retreated.

"It's still right outside. I don't think we can get close enough to the hole to fill it back in," said Osaze.

"It doesn't appear to help much, anyway," said Nour.

The bugs were gone. So were the sounds of growling. So far, each plague lasted an entire week. Why had that one been diff...oh! Others in the house were waking up with looks of surprise, bewilderment, astonishment, and contemplation. Even the animals in the pit had disappeared without a trace.

"Thank you so much for letting us stay," said Selma.

"Of course, we weren't going to leave you to the beasts," Lapis replied.

"We should check on our friends and neighbors to see if they're okay," Osaze suggested, "also if they've seen Jabari."

Almost every house they passed had at least part of a wall destroyed. Many had entire walls or roofs that collapsed.

"Osaze!" They turned around to see Bes carrying his wife, Layla, followed by Kesi and Omorose. Along with the standard bites and stings, they were covered in scratches.

"Is she okay?" Madu asked.

"She was passed out for a few hours, but it looks like she'll survive," Bes informed.

"Have you seen Jabari?" Nour asked.

They shook their heads.

Madu couldn't believe her eyes when she saw Jabari, face slightly swollen, walking towards the house!

"You're all alive!" he cheered.

"We sheltered with another family," Selma explained, locking him in an embrace. "Where have you been?"

"I made it to another roof. I spent the last hour with Hasina's family."

"How are they?" Nour asked.

Jabari took a deep breath, closed his eyes, barely getting out the words, "she was killed."

"Hasina couldn't outrun the wolf!" Tears streamed down Sabra's face.

"We saw someone die right in front of us!" said Nour, putting an arm around him.

"He almost took down a wolf. Without him, I wouldn't have made it onto the roof to safety. It got back up and attacked almost immediately," said Madu.

"We lost Jabari and went a full day not knowing he was alive!"

"He thought you were right behind him. He was terrified," Sabra said.

"We had many close calls," Madu told him, "I'm sure you did, too."

"Mom's been doing much better! She's on her feet again, but she's still in pain, and light-headed from blood loss," Kesi informed.

"That's a relief!" said Madu.

"Thanks for checking in! There's a ton of work to be done! So much was destroyed by the beasts and now the cattle aren't doing so well."

"What's wrong with the cattle?"

"Their mouths and noses are riddled with lesions, they're drinking excessive amounts of water, let's see, they seem to be having trouble breathing, they're salivating pretty heavily, oh, and they smell terrible!"

Madu raised an eyebrow. "And they all started showing these symptoms today?"

"We've been distracted these last few days, but yes. We just noticed that they're all sick."

Madu nodded. "I should check on ours."

Madu's fears were confirmed when she realized every single one of her family's cows showed these exact symptoms.

The crowd had grown considerably since the last protest. Hasina's whole family was there, even Hathor and Kafele, who claimed they couldn't care less about politics.

A woman with polished make-up and ruby sandals emerged from the palace. Madu gasped. They had caught the attention of Neema, Pharaoh's head mistress. "Hi everyone, I'm so glad to see you kids standing up for what is right! Pharaoh's actually already been doing so much to fight the plagues! The magicians are working on counter-spells. I have as many bug bites as the rest of you, and my heart goes out to everyone who lost their lives! Luckily, the wild animals are gone! Pharaoh's trying to convince Moses to back down from the deal."

"Moses made it clear what the conditions are. As for the magicians, they know they're powerless against the plagues! The only way to prevent more plagues is to set the Hebrews free!" Hasina and Sabra's mom, Rashida demanded.

"I don't really know much about magic," Neema admitted, "but we're not freeing the slaves."

"My daughter was killed by a wolf! Freeing the slaves would prevent who knows how many more deaths!"

"This is a good learning opportunity," said a man passing by. He gestured to Rashida. "Here's how adults shouldn't be acting. She's leading you children astray.

Instead of attacking the other side, we need to listen to each other."

"But you're throwing our future away!" Madu exclaimed.

Neema handed out cards. "Here's how to reach me. Thanks for stopping by!"

"Would you like to come with us to the protest?" Madu asked her father.

Osaze sighed. "I'm going to pass. Honestly, I don't know what to think!"

"Just a few days ago, you told me Pharaoh would be crazy not to set the Hebrews free!"

"I did think that at the moment. Now that the cattle are sick, I'm even more worried about getting by economically."

"Do you think setting the Hebrews free will set us back further than the plagues will?"

"I don't know. I really don't know!" He added, "if you're going to protest, just please do it peacefully."

"Of course! For the record, we're not only demanding that the slaves be set free. We're also fighting for the needs of the lower class," Madu added.

"You're asking for quite a lot!" Osaze chuckled.

"I know," Madu responded. "But anything less won't be nearly enough."

"I get it. I understand the stance you're taking. I just need some time."

Madu nodded. They didn't have a lot of time, but she would let him have some.

Madu had long enjoyed painting on roofs in her free time. Today, she painted on the remnants of a wall in the busy part of the city. Hasina's eyes focused on the onlooker. Her mouth wasn't quite a smile and not quite a frown. Her shoulders were down. She looked ready to take it on and was inviting the onlooker to join. Below, Nour had written: "Justice for Hasina."

He read Madu the list of names on the pillar.

Massika, daughter of Habibah and Akil
Chibale, high priest
The healer, Maat, daughter of Nawa
The teacher, Keket, daughter of Zaim and Gamila
Amsu, son of Comter and Dakarai
Psamatic, military scribe
The artist, Tefnut
Radamas, son of Omari
Aseneth, daughter of Hu and Ebonee
Kissa, high priestess
Hasina, daughter of Rashida and Gamal
The ferryman, Saa, son of Shani and Zane

Odion, son of Nubia

Fukayna, daughter of Kek and Ini-Herit

The potter, Tau, son of Udele and Maged

When they turned around, they saw that a crowd had gathered. They carried signs, ready to march and demand change.

As impressive as the turnouts were, there were also people actively avoiding them. They barricaded their windows in fear of violence. Rumors spread of angry, violent protests and the disruptions they caused. Madu only sighed as she watched two women grow fearful looks on their faces and do a one-eighty in the other direction.

As they marched, government horses galloped towards them. As they got closer, it became apparent that they weren't going to ride by the protesters, but instead charged into the mass! As people tried to avoid being trampled, officials threw painful dust into the crowd, irritating their eyes.

They hadn't been able to get the cattle to do any work all day. They've been lying in the shade. They tried their best to treat them, but it was a lost cause.

After the protest, Madu, Nour, and Jabari came to check on them. None of them had moved. They nudged them.

"This one's not responding," said Jabari. There were already flies circling, which didn't seem noteworthy to them. They couldn't find a pulse, and the cow didn't appear to be breathing.

"Kids, we're going to need you to help us tomorrow. Without cows to graze, we'll need to do it ourselves," Osaze announced.

"What do you think tomorrow will be like?" Selma inquired.

"A lot of work," said Madu, heading inside.

Boils

It wasn't just bug bites anymore. Some were almost triple in size. Dry skin surrounded the reddish-white bumps. Madu thought her bug bites had hurt, but now the pain was excruciating! Without cattle, Osaze, Bes, and Nour cut the furrows with the heavy plow. They were followed by Madu and Kesi turning the soil with the light plow. Jabari and Omorose sprinkled the seeds into the furrows. Layla and Selma used hoes to sow the seeds and break up smaller clumps of soil.

After the seeds were planted, they used the shaduf to water them. A large pole was balanced on a cross-beam. One end had a rope and a bucket, and the other had a counter-weight. Madu pulled the rope and lowered the bucket into the water. Then, Nour pulled down on the weight and raised the bucket. He swung the pole around to water the crops.

All day, the hot sun beat down on them. They'd spent long days in the field before, but the heat was irritating their skin to a much worse degree than normal. Madu's skin was flaky and blistery. Were the bumps still growing? She had to get out of the sun. But there was still so much work to do. Madu didn't want to pull the plow. She didn't want to bend over a hoe either. She didn't want to feel anything on her skin.

Pharaoh didn't have to work in the blazing sun. He had people to take care of the fields for him.

Off in the distance, she saw someone watching them at work. Did they not have anything better to do? Madu realized that this was Rabiah, the woman she met in the market, and decided to approach her.

"I've been thinking about what you said," Rabiah said, "You said that poor people are worried about getting by if the slaves are freed. But the plagues seem to be affecting poor people most anyway."

"It's not so easy to come to terms with being stuck in a lose-lose-situation."

"I see," Rabiah replied, face unwavering.

"But the fact is, we are. Once we acknowledge that, we have to look beyond. We must look into why we're in the lose-lose situation to begin with. We can't just ask Pharaoh to pick a side; we need him to find a different solution altogether to fix the actual problem."

After the work was done, Madu waited while her parents discussed marriage with Ebo. At last, he met her by the Nile.

"How'd it go?"

"They think we're a good match! It's not the right time for marriage, though."

"That's what I was thinking."

They held hands and walked along the river. Ebo's family needed to get back on their feet before he could provide for her.

He looked at her. "When this is all over, we are going to get married," he said.

When this is all over.

"Stay inside! Stay inside! If you go outside, you WILL get struck by lightning and die! Bring in your animals!" A messenger ran around yelling.

"Sounds like we should all be heading home!" Madu and Kesi had been babysitting Jabari and Jumoke.

"Those guys over there don't seem to be paying attention," Jumoke noticed.

"The hail probably doesn't start until tomorrow," said Jabari.

"Seems wise to head in now, so that we can bring in the animals and make sure we have enough food in the house," said Madu.

That's what they saw others doing. A few groups of people seemed to think they could wait it out.

"See you in two to seven days!"

Selma, Osaze, and Nour had brought in all the goats, pigs, ducks, and geese. They harvested extra crops.

Selma had insisted on gathering all the leaves she could for wiping.

Madu looked out the window. She frowned. "Get inside! You're in danger!'

Outside, they rolled their eyes. "Don't tell us what to do!" someone muttered.

Hail

Thunder struck. Huge balls of ice assaulted the ground, accompanied by a trail of fire. Within seconds, every tree was down, every blade of grass incinerated!

It felt like the end. There was no running from the storm. It hit everything. Their walls had been repaired as best they could since the beasts, but they worried they weren't sturdy enough.

Nour happened to be finishing class when the message went out. His teacher had assigned work to do at home.

Everyone else passed the time playing a game of Mehen. At the moment, the focus wasn't on the hail, or anything they were missing by staying inside. The goal was being the first to move their marbles to the center of the coiled snake. Jabari was the one to accomplish this, but he didn't have any ones stored up. Osaze followed close behind and rolled two ones right away, unleashing the lion. Jabari, Selma, and Madu dodged as many of their marbles as they could.

When the game was done, hail was still falling. Plants were still catching fire. It was fortunate that they gathered their crops when they did.

"What are they doing?" Little by little, people were coming out of their homes, most carrying leafy umbrellas. They ran into each other, hugged, and said hello. No one lasted long.

"I think they're just tired of staying inside," said Selma.

To their great dismay, the umbrellas weren't suitable shelter. When hail so much as brushed past, every leaf caught fire in milliseconds, lost structure, and fell on the person. Even without umbrellas, every fallen body became kindling. The more people going out, the longer the fires stayed on the ground, the more they spread, the more they grew. The people going outside weren't just choosing unwisely for themselves; they were putting everyone in danger!

The good news was that it remained safe inside. As long as there were walls on all sides and a roof, they were protected. Madu was so grateful they'd gotten around to repairing theirs! Their main worry now was the height of the fires. Luckily, for now they were still relatively low. Madu was much more worried about one of the houses she saw in the distance. An entire corner, almost two walls, were destroyed along with a good chunk of roof. Madu hoped that the people inside had found somewhere else for the time being.

"Look at you, standing around, staring out a window," Nour teased. "I challenge you to a Mehen rematch!"

Madu grinned. "Bring it on!"

With Madu's guidance, Jabari was getting better at milking the goats. He smiled at the full bucket. A goose swooped down, and Jabari quickly covered it.

"Nice work!" Madu set the bucket on the table, where at least the pigs or goats wouldn't knock it over.

"Of course I'll wait, but eventually, I might have to!" she heard Osaze quietly tell Selma.

"No less than a week! You know that people are dying!" said Selma.

"Our family's going to starve if I'm not out there selling!"

"You want to go out in the hail?" Madu exclaimed.

"I don't *want* to."

"You aren't going to sell anything," said Madu.

"No plague has lasted more than seven days. I doubt it will come to this," said Selma.

"We shouldn't have to consider going outside," said Nour.

Locusts

More bugs. Not a patch of land went uncovered by locusts. The efforts that they made to harvest crops at the last minute had been a lost cause. Being spared by the hail meant nothing.

"The barley was in the ear and the flax was in bud. The wheat and emmer aren't ready yet. Hopefully, the locusts won't be around then," Osaze explained, though he knew that they weren't far behind.

Life returned to as close to normal as it could be. It was safe to go outside again. Nour went back to school. Protests could resume.

Madu couldn't see the people who had died the day before. The sea of locusts covered up the brutal reminder of the horror, the tragedy, the cost. How different things would have been had they been confronted with it, by walking past bodies or piles of ashes.

Playing outside in the neighborhood, Madu, Nour, Sabra, and Kesi looked up from their game when they heard chants for freedom.

"Enough is enough!"

"Slaves were meant to be slaves!"

"Make Egypt great again!"

Kesi gasped. "They can't do that!"

"Is that the list of names?!" Madu cried, "what are they writing over it?!"

Nour and Sabra squinted, trying to see past the locusts. Sabra put his head in his hands.

"Hoax?" Nour answered.

Madu understood people like her father worrying about their families, but how could anyone with any human decency do this? Had these people always had such anemic compassion?

They were starving. The decision to kill an animal was a tough one. The eggs were a first priority, since they were there and ready to eat. Some had to be fertilized. They had to eat them sparingly, but before they went bad. They had to prioritize animals that were past their reproductive prime. When they did kill one, that meant a lot of meat at once before going back to days of nothing. The family had been eating eggs pretty much as fast as they were laid, and thought maybe it was time for meat. They didn't know how long they'd have to apportion out what they had. Nor did they know if or when they'd lose access.

Darkness

Madu woke up in the middle of the night. She lay awake for some time before realizing that she wasn't tired enough to sleep. Her stomach growled. She figured her hunger was keeping her up. She considered going for a walk but wasn't sure it was a good idea. The locusts were gone, so anything could be out there. Best to wait until morning.

Someone stepped on her leg. Madu yelped.

"Sorry!"

"Mom? What are you doing up?"

"I couldn't sleep," Selma answered."

"Where are you going?"

"To check on the animals."

Madu followed her outside. She walked until she touched the wall. She continued until she found the door.

There was no moon visible nor starlight. She heard animal noises, nothing out of the ordinary.

Something brushed past her. Madu guessed it to be one of their animals.

"Mom, how are you planning on checking on them?"

"You followed me out here? I thought you would go back to sleep."

"They seem fine," said a male voice who sounded like Osaze. "It's hard to tell for sure, but as far as I know, they're all here in good health. We have plenty of geese of each sex. We're all hungry enough that we can afford to eat some meat now."

"We should wait until morning," said Madu.

"She's right; the sun should come up soon. Then, we can get an idea of the age, sex, and size. Plus, it'll be much easier to butcher it!"

"You're the one who told me to come out here!"

"I haven't spoken to you since waking up!"

"Oh, I see. Your mother and I decided we should eat some fresh meat." He sounded like he was walking away.

"The house is the other way," said Madu. "Walk towards my voice."

"Madu, that's not your father," said Selma.

"Well, he's taking one of our geese!"

They ran after him.

"Give that back to us!" Madu demanded.

"Madu?"

"Bes?"

"We thought you were stealing our goose!"

"I thought this was my goose. But you can come in while we wait for morning."

Morning never came. Madu felt like she had a full night of sleep. Bes' family hadn't killed any animals the past few days.

"Does anyone know where a knife is?" Bes asked.

Madu felt the surface of a table, not finding anything.

"I found something, but it's a little dull. We can try it if we can't find anything sharper."

"This is sharp."

"Great! Follow the sound of my voice."

Someone crashed into something.

"I lost it! Here it is," A moment later, "I think I feel feathers."

Once the goose was killed, they needed to figure out how to cook it. They searched the ground for rock, flint, anything to start a fire. At last, one rock was found, then another. They roasted the goose over as big a fire as they could.

Madu had wondered whether it was the sun, moon, and stars being impacted, or if it was their own eyes directly. They had to rely on abstract knowledge to know who they were with, where everything was, and what they were doing. They couldn't rely on anything more than theoretical reason for what should be happening. Now, when they rubbed two rocks together, they saw the flames exactly as they expected. Their eyes were working perfectly.

"It feels cooked." She held the meat close to the fire. "I think it's cooked through."

Madu chose not to eat since she ate yesterday. Selma, still thinking the goose was theirs, let them serve her some.

"This is raw!"

"This is very cooked!"

"Mom, Madu, are you over there?"

"Yes, bring your father and brother over."

"Jabari knocked over-"

"It was Nour!"

"Someone knocked over a big canister of water, so we tried to get more. On our way to the Nile, we were attacked by a mob, possibly protesters."

"There have been protests against freeing the slaves. What they're hoping to accomplish, I don't think they know," Madu explained.

"Or, this was a protest *for* freeing the slaves!"

"Did you get the water?"

"No, we didn't want to risk it."

"The market's supposed to be open tomorrow," Osaze announced.

"You're going to go out and sell?"

"How will they see what they're buying?"

"We'll learn to manage. We'll learn to live without light. Perhaps it'll be a matter of waiting for our vision to adjust."

"You think we'll learn to see in the dark?"

Madu opened her mouth but didn't say anything. She'd been through it before, doing what she could to inform them. It wasn't worth it. If they wouldn't listen, that was on them.

She stood up. She'd heard enough foolishness. Some people will tell themselves anything to avoid changing their minds.

Cautiously, she made her way to the wall, then to the door, then found her way out.

Madu's hope was that she would find her own house, but her expectations weren't definite. She'd walked this distance often enough times to have a feel for it.

Turn here.

She walked a few more paces. She should have arrived by now. She was surely only a few paces away. But in which direction? She turned left and walked a bit more until she had to have passed it. She turned left again, walked, and turned left again.

She walked a little further than her original estimate. After more turns and recalculations, she found a wall. She traced the wall until it ended. The wall-less space was too wide to be a door, so Madu traced the other way. At last, she found it.

"Is someone there?"

Madu froze.

"What if it's *them* again!?"

"We're armed!"

"What if it's not them?"

"Then they made an awfully rash decision to leave their house!"

Madu backed away quietly.

"Selma! Nour! Kesi!" Madu called, "it's Madu!"

"Madu, it's me, Omorose!"

Madu walked her direction. She had found her way back.

"Where are you?"

"Over here!"

Madu found her way back in.

"Where were you?"

"I needed to step out."

"That's surprising."

"I wouldn't recommend it," Madu warned.

"We can't hunker down forever."

"Was that you, Dad?" asked a male voice.

"Yes, that was me."

"Well, you're being hypocritical."

"Excuse me!?"

"You've been going on and on about needing to proceed with our lives. They're in shambles, and you know it! We know what needs to be done! It's been clearly stated since the beginning. You've just pretended not to hear!"

Madu chimed in. "Everyone was uncertain in the beginning. Things were changing, and we had a lot to wrap our heads around. We have financial worries being affected by freeing the slaves and also by the plagues. You see how things could get worse, but not how things are already getting worse! After the frogs disappeared, you assumed everything was right despite knowing the rules. You insisted on going to the market despite the darkness or the hail that would have killed you as soon as you stepped outside. You accused our protests of being violent, overlooking the violence of the government's response and the counter protests! We've told you the extent to which we've been protesting! We've told you how we're demanding that Pharoah meet our economic needs, but you ignore that part! You're stubborn, Dad, stubborn, delusional, and outright stupid!"

Death of the First-born Sons

There was light when Madu woke up. She sat up and blinked a couple of times. Layla offered a big canister of water. Having barely drank these past couple of days, Madu gulped some down and passed it to Jabari.

The house was waking up, hugging, and wishing one another good morning. Madu wanted to apologize to her dad. She should have said it differently. She shouldn't have called him stupid.

He and Nour were the only ones who hadn't gotten up.

"Dad, are you awake?"

"Let him sleep, his sleep cycle's probably a little off," Selma told her.

His skin felt cool. His eyes and mouth were open. His pupils were dilated. He wasn't breathing.

She looked up to see Jabari, gazing at Osaze with wide eyes.

"Is he…" Omorose looked from Madu to Jabari to Osaze to Nour. "And he…"

Kesi knelt beside Nour and searched for a pulse. She nodded, eyes downcast.

Jabari sat down and put his head in his hands. Madu put her arms around him.

They had just dropped dead overnight. Osaze, Nour, Jumoke, Ebo, Sabra. Everyone had someone to mourn.

Madu watched the pristine river flow. She listened to the sounds of rushing water, birds, and people out and about. She felt sun against her skin and sand beneath her feet. She walked along undisturbed by anyone or anything. She took a deep breath.

She had lost so much. She didn't know how they would proceed. She wanted to spend the rest of her life listening to the river. But she knew that would be foolish.

Madu found a rock to sit on. Soon enough, Jabari came and sat next to her, shortly followed by Selma.

"Did you hear?" Selma asked, "Pharaoh set the Hebrews free."

Madu nodded. The three of them held hands. She took another deep breath.

Blood.
Frogs.
Lice.
Beasts.
Cattle disease.
Boils.
Hail.

Locusts.
Darkness.
Death of the first-born sons.

That was what it took.

Works Cited

(2009, February 12). Salmonella infections in cats. *Pet MD*. https://www.petmd.com/cat/conditions/digestive/c ct_salmonellosis

(2018, November 16). Scribes in Ancient Egypt. *Worldhistory.us*. https://worldhistory.us/ancient-history/ancient-egypt/scribes-in-ancient-egypt.php

(2018, November 21). Funerals in Ancient Egypt. *Australian museum.* https://australian.museum/learn/cultures/internatio nal-collection/ancient-egyptian/funeral s-in-ancient-egypt

(2019, July 21). The plague of frogs. *KJV bible truth.* https://www.kjvbibletruth.com/2019/07/21/the-plague-of-frogs/

(2020). *History of umbrella and parasol.* www.umbrellahistory.net

Agriculture in Ancient Egypt, irrigation tools and techniques of farming. *Egypt guide.* https://www.egyptprivatetourguide.com/egyptian-facts/agriculture-ancient-egypt-irrigati on-techniques-of-farming/

Ancient Egyptian farming, Ancient Egypt agriculture: seasons, techniques, animals, crops. *Facts about*

Ancient Egyptians.
https://ancientegyptianfacts.com/ancient-egyptian-farming.html

Ancient Egyptian games. *Ancient Egypt online*.
https://www.ancient-egypt-online.com/ancient-egypt-games.html

Ancient Egyptian pottery. *Egyptian eye*.
https://egyptianeye.net/egyptian-pottery/

Barrow, M. (2013). Ancient Egyptian farming. *Homework help*.
www.primaryhomeworkhelp.co.uk/egypt/farming.htm

Bower, B. (Program Director), Frey, W. (Program Author), Shafsky, K. (Creative Development Manager), Bergez, J. (Writer), Falstein, M. (Writer), Hart, D. (Writer), Howard, M. A. (Writer), Joseph, A. (Writer) (2011). Daily life in Ancient Egypt. In L. Alavosus (Ed.), *History alive!: The ancient world* (pp. 91-103). Teachers' Curriculum Institute 978-1-58371-901-5

Crispe, S. E. (2013, March 7). The lice infestation. *Chabad.org*.
https://www.chabad.org/blogs/blog_cdo/aid/2129271/jewish/The-Lice-Infestation.htm

Egyptian farming. *History for kids*.
https://www.historyforkids.net/egyptian-farming.html

Egyptian food. *History for kids*.
https://www.historyforkids.net/egyptian-food.html

Egyptian games. *History for kids*.
https://www.historyforkids.net/ancient-egytpian-games.html

Egyptian names. *Disney family*.
https://family.disney.com/baby-names/egyptian-names/

Exodus. In *The five books of Moses* (2nd ed.). (1999). The Jewish Publication Society. (Original   work published in 1962).

Farming in Ancient Egypt [PowerPoint slides]. Primary resources .co.uk.
www.primaryresources.co.uk/google_search.htmx=partner-pub6473552687555565%3A224358&cof=FORID%3A10%ie=UTF-8&q=farming+in+ancient+egypt&sa=Search

FSSL. (2015, May 21). The plagues of Egypt: Lesson 9: The plague of boils. *Free Sunday school lessons*.
https://www.freesundayschoollessons.org/?s=the+plagues+of+egypt%3A+the+plague+of+boils

Gugliada, L. (2019, January 03). Papyrus plant dates
back to Ancient Egypt. *Silive.com.*
https://www.silive.com/homegarden/garden/2011/
02/papyrus-plants-dates-back-to-an.html

Homyden. (2017, August 05). When do plum trees
bloom? *Homyden.* https://homyden.com/when-do-
plum-trees-bloom/

Howard, J. The flowers of Ancient Egypt and today.
Tour Egypt.
www.touregypt.net/featurestories/flowers.htm

James. Facts about ancient egyptian pets. *Primary facts.*
https://www.priamryfacts.com/80/facts-about-
ancient-egyptian-pets/

Jcromwell. (2020, May 27). Caring for cows in Ancient
Egypt. *Papyrus stories.* https://papyrus-
stories.com/2020/05/27/caring-for-cows-in-
ancient-egypt/

Kile, J. How to play the Ancient Egyptian board game of
mehen. *All about fun and games*
https://allaboutfunandgames.com/how-to-play-the-
ancient-egyptian-board-game-of-meh_en

Mark, J. J. (2013, January 19). Ancient Egyptian burial.
Ancient history encyclopedia.
https://www.ancient.eu/artciel/Egytpian_Burial/

Mark, J. J. (2016, March 18). Pets in Ancient Egypt.
Ancient history encyclopedia.

https://www.ancient.eu/article/875/pets-in-ancient-egypt/

Mark, J. J. (2016, April 01). The lamentations of Isis and Nephthys. *Ancient history encyclopedia.* https://www.ancient.eu/article/878/the-lamentations-of-isis-and-nephthys/

Mark, J. J. (2016, September 21). Daily life in Ancient Egypt. *Ancient history encyclopedia.* https://www.ancient.eu/article/933/daily-life-in-ancient-egypt/

Mark, J. J. (2017, January 08). Color in Ancient Egypt. *Ancient history encyclopedia.* https://www.ancient.eu/article/999/color-in-ancient-egypt/

Mark, J. J. (2017, March 16). Beer in Ancient Egypt. *Ancient history encyclopedia.* https://www.ancient.eu/article/1033/beer-in-ancient-egypt/

Marriage in Ancient Egypt. *Ancient Egypt online.* https://www.ancient-egypt-online.com/ancient-egypt-marriage.html

Measurement conversions. *Ancient history encyclopedia.* https://www.ancient.eu/measure/

Michelle. (2016, June 16). How to tell if a plum is ripe. *Just plums.*

https://justplums.blogspot.com/2011/06/how-to-tell-if-a-plum-is-ripe.html

Pariona, A. (2018, January 26). Amphibian species of Egypt. *World Atlas*. https://www.worldatlas.com/articles/amphibian-species-of-egypt.html

Pina-Dacier, M. (2015, June 17). This Ancient Egyptian process purifies dirty water. *Digventures*. https://digventures.com/2015/06/this-ancient-egyptian-process-purifies-dirty-water/

Posner, M. What was the fourth plague? *Chabad.org*. https://www.chabad.org/parshah/article_cdo/aid/1398412/jewish/What-Was-the-Fourth-Plague.htm

Raymond, C. (2020, September 18). What physically happens to your body right after death. *Verywell health*. https://www.verywellhealth.com/what-happens-to-my-body-right-after-i-die-1132498

Rinderpest. *Encyclopedia Britannica*. https://www.britannica.com/science/rinderpest

Rosmorduc, S. (2018, June 08). How were Ancient Egyptian last names chosen? *Quora*. https://www.quora.com/How-were-Ancient-Eygyptian-last-names-chosen

The fourth plague: Wild beasts/flies. *Mazornet*.

https://mazornet.com/mazornet/holidays/Passover/
plagues/flies.htm

The importance and significance of cats in Ancient
Egypt. *Historyplex*.
https://historyplex.com/signicance-of-cats-in-
ancient-egypt/

The sixth plague: Boils. *Mazornet*.
https://www.mazornet.com/mazornet/holidays/Pas
sover/plagues/boils.htm

The third plague: Lice. *Mazornet*.
https://www.mazornet.com/mazornet/holidays/Pas
sover/plagues/lice.htm

Weird History. (2019, March 10). *Ancient Egypt: What
everyday life was actually like* [Video]. Youtube.
https://www.youtube.com/watch?v=eQzHY13Q7Q